A Man for More Than A Season

Julia A. Royston

BK
ROYSTON
Publishing

BK Royston Publishing
P. O. Box 4321 | Jeffersonville, IN 47131
502-802-5385
http://www.bkroystonpublishing.com
bkroystonpublishing@gmail.com

Cover Design: Elite Cover Designs

ISBN-13: 978-1-955063-42-5

Printed in the United States of America

Dedication

To those who desire love for a life time and not just for one season.

Acknowledgements

First, I acknowledge my Lord and Savior Jesus Christ for giving me all of my gifts and especially my gift to write His words.

My husband who is always supportive, loving and encouraging me to utilize all of my gifts and talents. Thank you honey.

To my mother, Dr. Daisy Foree, who is my number one cheerleader and always tells me, "hang in there, you can do it." To my father, Dr. Jack Foree, who is never far away from me in spirit or my heart. I only have to look in the mirror each day to see him.

To Rev. Claude and Mrs. Lillie Royston who support me in everything I do.

To the rest of my family, I love you and thank you for your prayers, support and love.

To the team of BK Royston Publishing and Royal Media and Publishing that make it easier for me to write and publish the books I love, thank you!

Table of Contents

A Man for More Than A Season

The Season

The weather was cool and the trees had no leaves. It was that time again a season with no man. Matthew was the latest to leave and continue the trend. As it goes, after the Labor Day holiday, the calls stop and the dates cease. It happened so often Tamera came up with a slogan, 'it must be fall so he won't call, when it's spring my phone will ring.' It was depressing but, true. Over the past five years, Tamera dated only half of the year, spring and summer. When she needed a sweater, the man would scatter.

'Not another slogan', Tamera thought to herself as she headed down Main Street in the small town of Orleans, Kentucky. Orleans was a sister city of the big easy but, clearly located in the Bluegrass state.

The smooth jazz version of 'When will I see you again,' filled the car as she pondered, 'Is it too much to ask God for a date that will be around past October 1st?' There was total silence. At thirty-five, Tamera James was relatively attractive, pleasingly plump as her aunts would say, no kids, a librarian at the local public library and the best aunt two nieces and three nephews could ask for. Tamera had one sister and two brothers who were happily married and repopulating the earth. Her mother even remarried after her father passed away ten years ago. Now that was a little disturbing that her mother could marry and she could not.

At times, Tamera felt like she had some type of disease that drove men away. That couldn't be the case, because she attracted them for at least two seasons. There must be a sign posted on her back side that said available for dating only in spring and summer. Men watched her backside enough. If there were something posted on it, they would have noticed and told her about it as they read it out loud.

Somehow it was the same old story. A relatively attractive man walks into the library and approaches the cute librarian at the circulation desk.

Cute Librarian says, 'hello, can I help you find a book today?'

Handsome man says, 'yes, I am looking for the latest science fiction books.'

About four visits later, while returning library books, the handsome man uttered the awkward statement, 'maybe we can go out some time' or 'can I have your number so we can go out some time?

At other times he would say, 'Can you take a look at your schedule and let me know when you are free, so we can go out some time?' 'I will call you.'

'Sure,' said the cute librarian as she received the books and handed him her number. The dating game began. The season must now be spring.

The weather was hot and so was the relationship. They met each other's family, sometimes he begged to stay over and the phone never stopped ringing. Tamera was a good Christian girl but, sometimes the guy was so good that she wanted to cave in but, didn't. She knew that God would forgive her but, could she forgive herself. These thoughts always let Tamera know she was in over her head in heat, not love, and the season changed again, now it was summer. They were adults and kissing was never enough for either of them but, grandmamma taught her that 'she was the marrying kind and she was not the "have fun with and throw away" kind of girl.'

She kept her phone on vibrate during the day and full ring at night. There was nothing, not a call or even a voice mail. She knew the season had changed again. It was October 1st and now it is fall. Tamera always prayed that one day she would have a man in her life not just one or two seasons but, them all.

"What are you and Matthew doing for Thanksgiving?" Katherine, the Technical Services librarian asked, as she uploaded the latest acquisitions onto the library database.

"Who is Matthew?" Tamera's dry tone told details that her words didn't have to utter.

"What happened?" Katherine exclaimed, hushed but, forceful because they were in the library's main room.

"What happens every October 1st? Nothing. No calls, voice mails or dates. Everything stops." Tamera explained.

"Girl, I am so sorry. I thought he was really into you. He seemed like he liked you."

"They all do. He liked me. He said he did. His mama liked me. His daddy liked me. His sister and his brother like me. But, it is always suspicious that when the holidays roll around, nobody likes me. I didn't ask him for one gift. I am not a gold digger. I take care of all of my own stuff. I am not looking for a man to give me stuff but, love. Is that too much to ask?" Tamera waited with a stare that bordered on tears.

"No, it is not too much to ask. Hold on to that thought and don't settle until you get it."

"Well, I will probably be too old to meet him or enjoy it when he comes along."

"No, you will do just fine. I pray hard for you single girls every day."

"Right."

The Cocoa Brown Stranger

At that moment, a very tall, cocoa brown skinned man walked into the front door. Under her breath Katherine whispered, "Who is that tall, handsome glass of water and how did he get to Orleans. Tamera, girl, this could be your lucky day."

"He looks like something out of the movies. I am not that lucky," Tamera whispered under her breath.

"How can I help you?" Katherine spoke first and asked very sweetly.

"I am looking for the genealogy section," the young man stated.

"I am sorry but, I am not the reference librarian. I am the technical librarian but, I am sure that this young lady right here can help you." Katherine smiled to the gentleman and walked away quickly. Katherine was much taller than Tamera. On the stools at the Reference Desk, she could look directly into the gentleman's face with ease. Tamera needed a step stool for a direct view.

"Yes, sir. Let me get my keys. The genealogy section is in a closed room down the hall. I have to let you in the room. Is there a particular year that you are interested in?"

"I am looking for the birth records from 1978. I have been to the courthouse but, they tell me that you keep them here." Tamera found the keys easily. Darius Mathes stepped away from the desk allowing Tamera to get a whiff of the crisp fresh blue water cologne compared to the stale musty smell of the close genealogy room. Tamera was glad that, in spite of the way she felt, she still came to work looking professional and stylish.

"That is correct. The courthouse is not climate controlled so the records are kept here." Tamera spent time in the men's section of many department stores she thought she smelled 'Dolce and Gabanna Light Blue.' It was not too overwhelming and blended well with his natural body chemistry.

Tamera turned on the light as she walked only a few steps to the birth records. Opening a third drawer, she said, "Here are the records for the 1970's. They are arranged by year for every person that was born in Orleans or the surrounding three counties for any year. If you have any questions, pick up that phone right there and dial 118. The number is also located on top of the phone. If you exit this room the door automatically locks and you can't get back in without me or the key. Well, you could get in with the key but, I need to bring it or someone else could bring it to you. Sorry. I know I sound ridiculous. I will shut up now." Tamera realized how ridiculous she did sound and suddenly got tickled and so did he.

"I am sorry. I didn't mean to laugh at you but, you were laughing so it made me laugh. I got it. What's your name?"

"I'm Tamera. No problem, I get tickled when I am nervous."

"I am Duane Mathis and nice to meet you Tamera. I will need you and the keys for the next 3 days. I am staying here in town to do some research."

"Well, I will leave you to your research and if you need anything, there is the phone."

"Thanks Tamera."

"You are welcome, Mr. Matthis."

"Please call me Duane."

Duane

"Okay, Duane." Tamera dipped her head leaving the room with little fanfare and without bumping into anything as well. Tamera always seemed to get clumsy when she was nervous.

Duane Matthis came to the library's Genealogy Room for the next three days. Tamera enjoyed seeing him come through those doors each evening. No major conversation ensued but, general pleasantries were expressed. On the third night,

Duane stayed until the library closed.

Walking to the reference desk, he happily announced, "Tamera, I have found what I was looking for and thank you for all of your help."

Tamera surprised herself by being slightly saddened by the news.

She managed to say, "You are welcome. Have a nice evening." Looking at handsome Duane Matthes for three days had been a wonderful diversion from the usual men in the town who came to the library. Tamera watched as

Duane left the library continuing to prepare the library to close. The supplies were restocked and the desk was cleaned off and ready for the early morning shift.

Tamera bent to gather her bag and while hidden from view, heard a voice saying, "Excuse me Tamera." Tamera looked up and then popped up like Jack in the box.

"Oh, hi Duane. I thought you had gone?"

"Well, I had gone but, had an idea. This is my last night in town and I am going to dinner to celebrate my findings. Since you were so helpful, I was wondering if you would have dinner with me tonight to help me celebrate." Tamera was shocked that a man would ask her out, because it was October. This was the wrong season for her to have a date.

"Um, well……." Tamera paused to think for a moment.

Duane hurried to help her make her decision, "I realize that you don't really know me, but, I promise, dinner will be on me. I just don't want to eat alone tonight and it is my last night in town. Please?"

Tamera looked up into his eyes again and then down at her outfit. She realized that she looked okay for dinner with a stranger. "Okay. Sure, I will have dinner with you tonight to help you celebrate. I have to finish closing the library first."

"Great. Meet me at the Orleans Inn when you are finished. Thank you so much." Duane smiled excitedly and left the library. Tamera stopped straightening the desk and started straightening her mind and wardrobe. A date in October? This was unheard of for Tamera. She had to keep telling herself, 'this is just a dinner between two adults. Don't get happy. It means nothing. He was going to leave town the next day.'

The Orleans Inn

The Orleans Inn was a combination Mansion/Plantation/Bed and Breakfast. Breakfast was served for overnight guests. The Inn was open to the public for lunch and dinner.

The bell attached to the front door rang loudly to announce each visitor.

"Welcome to the Orleans Inn." The hostess was Ms. Nosey Nora, as most folks in town called her. Ms. Nora was looking down at the newspaper when Tamera opened the door. The little bell on the door and Ms. Nora looked up from her paper. "Oh hello. Tamera. What brings you to Orleans Inn?"

Realizing that Tamera rarely ate at the Orleans Inn it was a logical question by Ms. Nora. "Hello, Ms. Nora, I am having dinner with one of your guests this evening." Tamera hated that Ms. Nora was on duty, the gossip train was about to leave the station.

 "There is nobody here but, that gorgeous Duane Mathes," said Ms. Nora, looking shocked and bewildered. "Ugh, you are meeting him? The Lord must be smiling down on you today."

"Yes, he must." Tamera didn't have time for that woman's attitude today. She walked right past her and into the main room.

"I'm sorry. Right this way." Ms. Nora shuffled her feet to get ahead of Tamera to actually lead the way to Duane's table. Duane stood as Tamera approached. She tried to remain calm and told herself, 'no expectations. Just enjoy the dinner.'

"Hello and thanks for coming." said Duane who had changed into khaki pants and a blue blazer with sparkling gold buttons compared to the earlier jeans and t-shirt. Tamera exchanged her flats for heels which were in her car trunk. The heels made her two inches taller.

"Thanks for inviting me." Duane pulled out her chair and as Tamera sat down she took in his cologne one more time. The server came over to their table and their order was taken quickly. Small talk began and Tamera found out some wonderful things about Duane, including why he came to Orleans. He came to find his mother. She let him talk and didn't ask him the name of his mother. Orleans was a very small town. Tamera was quite sure that she would know her. Tonight she wasn't a librarian, researcher or one who answered anybody's questions. Just a girl eating dinner with a nice boy. She could hear the excitement in his voice and see the happiness in his eyes. Even though he had wonderful adoptive parents, he still wanted to meet his birth mother. He stopped talking about his findings and asked Tamera about herself, her interests and how she became a librarian. Duane asked about

Tamera's family as well. This was a big switch because most guys were trying to compliment her into some type of sexual action. His real interest in her was refreshing. Duane was a CPA who someday wanted to own his own accounting firm as well as a non-profit consulting firm for small businesses. People need advice prior to starting businesses and he really wanted to help people. Tamera thought his business ideas sounded wonderful. Being a public library librarian was definitely a public service and not about the money. She enjoyed helping people find information that changed their lives as well as support their love of reading. All of the dishes were cleared, only the half-empty water glasses remained because they declined coffee. She finally asked that all important question.

"So when are you going to see her?"

"I don't know yet. I need to go home tomorrow and I'll think and pray about it. I want to call her first and see if she even wants to meet me. I don't know. She might say no."

"Although we've just met, you seem like such a wonderful man. I can't imagine her not wanting to meet you and see how you turned out. At thirteen years old, she couldn't have taken care of you without a lot of help. I am sure that it was the hardest and most important decision she ever had to make."

"Could you have done it?"

"Me with a baby at thirteen? I was a baby at thirteen. Maybe I could, but only with family help. I am still old school. I want a husband and then children."

"I agree. I want a wife and then children." Fortunately, Tamera's chocolate brown skin hid her blushing because Duane looked at her without blinking as he made that statement. Something changed in the entire atmosphere after that statement. Tamera told herself, 'don't flinch, just breath. Go ahead and ask.'

She asked, "So why don't you have a wife and children? What's stopping you?"

"What's stopping me? Me. Even though I had wonderful adoptive parents all of my life, I didn't find out

I was adopted until age eighteen. I was applying for a passport and knew where my parents kept their insurance papers, etc. They were out of town and I found my adoption documents. My world crashed in on me. I knew then that I couldn't commit until I was complete or as complete as humanly possible. There were too many questions and too few answers. My parents were sorry, apologetic and so upset about how I found out that I dropped the issue of finding my birth mother until now. It never went away it was just delayed."

"Do you have a girlfriend or special lady in your life?"

"Yes and no."

"What does that mean?" Tamera pressed gently and waited for Duane's answer.

"Yes, this young lady is someone that I go out with occasionally. On the other hand, I have been totally honest with her about my commitment issues. I say no, because I have never fully connected with anyone on any deep level. My heart, body and mind were not 'all in' because I have this unsolved mystery in my life. I feel like I am a puzzle and there is still one piece missing."

Although this were their first time together, Tamera wanted to help Duane sort things out so she pushed again. "And, now?"

"Maybe." Duane's voice trailed off into a low whisper as he looked slightly out the window into the darkness.

Tamera let the word just linger in the air thinking 'Wow, at least he was honest. As honest as he could be.'

"I'm not going to keep you any longer. I am sure that you want to get home and rest from your long day at work." Duane suddenly pulled himself back to the present.

"It was a long day but, I enjoyed your company."

"I enjoyed your company as well. I really appreciate you coming out with me tonight on such short notice. You were so helpful and I just wanted to do something to show my appreciation. You ready?"

"Yes." Duane signed the check as Tamera grabbed her things. He walked Tamera to her car.

Once at the car, Duane stretched out his hand for hers and held it as he said, "Good night and have a safe journey home."

"Good night to you too and you have a safe journey home as well. I on the other hand, don't live that far." They both laughed and he watched her drive away until her car was out of sight. Tamera knew it because she watched him standing there through her rearview mirror.

Date Recap

The next day Tamera arrived to work a little earlier than usual in a wonderful mood wearing a bright colored blouse and matching skirt. "Look at you lady sunshine. How was dinner last night?" Katherine asked, as she approached the Reference Desk, as she did every morning, putting reference books away that had been cataloged. She was shocked that Katherine would know about last night. "How did you know I went out to dinner last night?"

"Did you forget how small this town is? Nosey Nora is my mom's aunt. Aunt Nora called my mom and then my mom called me. She said, 'it was evident that the two of you enjoyed each other's company.'

"How did she know that?" Tamera turned her head with an annoyed frown to Katherine so fast she almost got whiplash.

"She was watching you the entire night either from the kitchen or the sitting area adjacent to the main room."

"For real. There are no secrets or privacy to be had in this town. It doesn't matter, Nosey Nora will not ruin my day. Ms. Nora needs to go get her a life and not just try to live mine."

"Right. No, there is no privacy unless it is in a book and Nosey Nora is not the hostess at the restaurant, silly. So how was he? Did you have fun? Are you going to see him again? Did you give him your number?"

"Oh my goodness Katherine, you have asked four questions and I haven't even breathed to answer the first one. Question 1, he is wonderful. He is a great guy, gorgeous, spiritual and decent human being. Question 2, he made me laugh, think about some things seriously and reflect all at the same time. Question 3, I probably won't see him again or any time soon, since he doesn't live near here and has a girlfriend. Question 4, he didn't ask for my number, so I didn't offer it."

"Look at you all grown up, acting mature and like a non-desperate single woman. I am proud of you."

"You would be proud. He mentioned a wife and kids and I was excited until

I pushed the envelope, as I always do, and found out about a girlfriend. How stupid of me to ruin my fantasy that he was single."

Katherine couldn't help but, laugh at that statement. "Yeah, he might have a girlfriend but, at least, you broke the cycle of someone asking you out in the month of October. That is so great." The two continued talking and laughing most of the morning.

Trick or Treat

The upcoming weeks were filled with ghosts, goblins, pumpkins and scary stories during story time after school. Tamera wasn't thrilled with Halloween and was glad when all of that ended on November 1st. Duane ran across her mind a few times since that October night at the Orleans Inn. He could have contacted her by calling the library but, Tamera, 'why would he? He has a girlfriend.'

Around November 15, Katherine came by with her cute invitations to her family Thanksgiving Holiday dinner. Katherine was always inviting single, displaced or people with little or no family to join in with her family during the holidays. Tamera thought that was so admirable and people were always appreciative. Tamera had plenty of family. They decided to take a cruise over Thanksgiving break. She loved her family but, seeing everyone coupled up with someone just naturally turned Tamera into the nanny/babysitter. No thanks and not this holiday. So when Katherine passed out her beautifully hand written, calligraphy personalized, invitations with 'special surprise' included, Tamera knew that she had to be there.

"Well, here is your invitation Tamera."

"Thanks, Katherine."

"What are your plans this Thanksgiving?"

"I really don't have any and getting this invitation is going to save me from being home alone with a frozen turkey dinner, hot chocolate and the beginning of the Christmas movies playing on the Hallmark channel."

"I'll have none of that. You will be with me and my family this Thanksgiving."

"What do you want me to bring?"

"Well, don't worry about cooking anything, just bring a couple of bottles of sparkling cider." Katherine said

"Sounds good to me. I'll come a little early to help out." Tamera was happy that she would be alone.

"Great." Katherine said.

The Holidays

It was amazing how Katherine enjoyed the holidays. She talked non-stop about everything happening during the holidays from the menu items, decorations, invitations and even activities that would happen throughout each day. Katherine was getting more excited about the holidays even though they were still a few weeks away. Tamera usually stopped by Katherine's house on holidays even when her own family came to visit. Tamera's holidays weren't much fun without a date but Katherine's house was always a buzz filled with the banter, fun, laughter and love that Tamera always saw and felt when she spent time with Katherine's family.

Katherine's excitement rubbed off on Tamera and she arrived early as planned to help Katherine in any way possible. She had called her family and they were enjoying 80 degree weather in Mexico. Tamera looked cute in her sweater, matching leggings, gold jewelry and flawless makeup. Tamera carried in two bottles of sparkling cider and a *Kern's Kentucky Derby* pie for dessert, her personal favorite. Katherine's niece opened the door, took her wrap and ushered her to the main room of the day, the kitchen.

"Hey, Tamera. So glad that you could come." Katherine greeted Tamera as she walked in the kitchen. Katherine was dressed in a very festive sweater and leggings with an apron that read 'kiss the cook.' It was evident of all of the hard work that went into preparing for this holiday. The detail in house was decorated to time, money and love. The wonderful smells coming from the kitchen made Tamera's mouth water with anticipation.

"Thanks for inviting me. What can I do to help?" Tamera asked Katherine as she laid her pie and bottles of sparkling wine on the counter.

"Nothing really, just keep me company, unless you want to go watch football."

"No, I am fine right here."

As usual the house was divided by function of room, age groups and activities. Some boys were outside shooting hoops. The girls were upstairs messing with Katherine's daughter's clothes and makeup. The men had the TV and remote in their full control_in the family room. The women were controlling the kitchen, as the guests continued to arrive with more food, dessert and other specialties. It was a food lover's paradise. Thanksgiving was about being thankful but, also a day for family, fun, football and yes, the best and most food in one place. Katherine's mother came in the kitchen and said that they were still waiting on one special guest to arrive and then dinner would be served. Katherine eyed Tamera and gave an agreeable, 'yes mother,' from the side of her mouth. Although, the meal was held at Katherine's house, Katherine's mother, Edna, always seemed to be in charge. Katherine gladly let her be in charge.

The Special Guest

When the doorbell rang, Katherine's mother, Edna, put both hands at her mouth, burst into tears and whispered, "He's here." I was concerned when I saw Ms. Edna overcome by so much emotion and watched for Katherine's reaction. Katherine gently put one arm around her mother and kissed her on the forehead whispering, "Mom, get the door. He's finally here." Ms. Edna leaped quickly from the kitchen bar stool and said out loud this time, "he's finally here." She was almost gliding down the hallway toward the door.

Katherine announced to everyone, "He's here and let's meet in the living room." All of the family seemed to know exactly what to do except Tamera. She was clueless.

Bewildered, Tamera caught up with Katherine to ask, "Katherine, who's here?" Katherine refused and did not give the secret away to Tamera, even though she was one of her closest friends.

"You'll find out in a minute." Katherine touched

Tamera's elbow assuredly as they moved down the short hallway to the living room. The kids were running in from outside, the basement and from the upstairs bedrooms to meet the special guest.

Standing in the back of the living room, Tamera wasn't able to see the guest very well. Since she was shorter than most of Katherine's family, she waited in the corner until the guest came her way. Halfway, into the living room, she looked up and realized that the special guest was Duane Mathes. Ms. Edna hugging him very tightly. All Tamera could think were two things, 'Ms. Edna is Duane's mother? Did you ever think about me?' She was surprised and happy to see him but, slightly miffed that he didn't call her.

Before her question could be answered, there was an announcement from Katherine's mother, Ms. Edna. "I know that some of you have heard my story but, let me tell you the abbreviated version right now. Fifty years ago, I was thirteen years old scared and found out I was pregnant by a fifteen year old boy in my neighborhood. My mother said that since my father was gone she couldn't afford to take care of any more kids so she sent me to my grandmother and they arranged to put my baby up for adoption. The hardest thing I ever had to do was carry that child for nine months but, I never saw or named him." Ms. Edna's voice broke for just a minute and Duane held her hand tighter. One of Katherine's sisters came close for support. There was not a dry eye in the room, including the men. She finally continued. "I am sorry. I get so emotional thinking about it. They put me to sleep and when I woke up, he was gone. I was never to mention it again. I came back to Orleans and it was over. No questions asked. What I didn't know was that she made the adoption closed so I could not find out where my baby was after he was adopted. I was a minor and she controlled everything. Since I had no name and did not know whether it was a boy or girl, I couldn't find him. About a month ago, my baby found me. I had always wondered what happened to my baby. Now, I know. He is a handsome young man." Her tears began again. "I am most thankful that he agreed to come spend Thanksgiving with us. Duane would you like to say something?"

"Yes, just that I thank you all for welcoming me with open arms. I look forward to many more holidays together. I appreciate it." Ms. Edna broke down again with tears of joy. She was truly humbled and grateful. Katherine had another brother. The entire family welcomed Duane with hugs, tears and introductions. Tamera cried as well. She cried for Katherine, her mom and seeing a family reunited. It was wonderful. What a Thanksgiving!

Duane finally made his way to Tamera. "Hi, how are you?"

"I am fine. How are you?"

"Great now. I met my mom, my other siblings and I am so glad to see you."

"It is good to see you again as well. All I can say is wow and congratulations. "

"Thank you. I prayed about seeing my birth mother and here is the result."

"Fantastic! I had no idea that I would see you on Thanksgiving."

"I know you didn't but, I did."

"How?"

"A little birdie told me."

Duane tilted his head slightly and motioned only with his eyes toward Katherine, who was walking past them.

"Oh, a little birdie told you, huh?"

"Yes." Katherine walked by with her head down smiling not making eye contact.

"Katherine, you knew and didn't tell me?"

"Well, no, I couldn't because I promised my mother. I love you Tamera but, I love my mother more and I promised. Are you surprised?"

"Triple surprised. I totally understand but, I will get even."

They both laughed and with a quick hug, Katherine winked while walking away. Duane and Tamera sat down on the bench seat at the window while he continued telling his story. The sun was going down behind the big oak tree reflecting its dimming light into the pond.

"I want you to know that I thought about you a lot over the past few weeks. I intended to call but, realized that I needed to take care of some things first before contacting you. As soon as I got back home though, a lot of things happened. The young woman I had been seeing broke up with me. She told me that she had reunited with an old boyfriend after attending a reunion. That relationship is officially over."

"Oh, I am sorry to hear that."

"I'm not. She deserved a whole man committed to her and that wasn't me."

"How long did you date her?"

"One year."

"Wow, that's something. I can't seem to date someone more than two seasons of the year."

"What?"

"Never mind, that's a long story for another time. What else happened?"

"The next day, my firm sent me on special assignment to China for 3 weeks."

"Congratulations that must have been great."

"It was great but, I left the same day that I arrived to work with no pre-planning I just packed up and left. When I returned, I was promoted to partner to open a branch of the firm in Branford, Kentucky."

"Our Branford, Kentucky?"

Duane held Tamera's gaze and said, "Now, it truly is our Branford,

Kentucky. I packed up my condo and moved to Branford last week."

"Really?" Tamera couldn't believe she said out load exactly what was going on in her head.

"Really. My adoptive parents aren't very happy that I won't be close to them but, happy that I won't be alone. I will be close to my other mom, my extended family and hopefully to you." Tamera felt a hot blush come on her face and she was thankful again for the chocolate skin to hide her reaction. She didn't have an answer but, was hopeful that she would have even more time to spend with Duane in the future. Just then Ms. Edna called out that dinner was ready to be served and eaten. Charles, Jr., who was the next oldest, led us in the blessing of the food.

Duane stood, reached out his hand to help Tamera of the bench and asked, "Are you ready for this?"

"Yes, I am." Hand in hand, the two made their way to Katherine's very crowded dining room. Tamera remained hopeful, that in her life, she could possibly have not only a man but this man for all seasons.

About the Author

Julia Royston spends her days doing what she loves, writing, publishing, speaking and coaching others to write and monetize their messages to the world.

"Helping You Get Your Message to the Masses and Turn Your Words into Wealth," that is her why and motto.

To date, Julia has written 63 books, recorded 3 music CDs and coached more than 250 to write and publish books as well as establish their own businesses.

She is the owner of five companies and a non-profit organization as well as the host of "Live Your Best Life" heard each Sunday morning at 10:00 a.m. EST/3:00 p.m. WAT. on www.envision-radio.com

To stay connected with Julia visit solo.to/juliaaroyston.

Other Books by Julia Royston